Zeppi

Zeppi is a born leader with lots of friends. He loves adventure!
Sometimes looking for excitement gets him in trouble. Zeppi is
great at every sport, but his favorite sport is basketball. Zeppi
loves to tell jokes and make people laugh.

Tora

Tora is the princess of the Fright family! She has perfect manners and loves to play with dolls. Tora also loves to tell her siblings what to do. Even though she can be bossy, Tora usually gives good advice. She always reminds her siblings to pray to God when they need help.

prayer monsters

Tora Fright Patches Things Up
A Story about Forgiveness

created by Tracey Madder

illustrated by Bonnie Pang

TYNDALE KIDS

Tyndale House Publishers, Inc.
Carol Stream, IL

Visit Tyndale's website for kids at www.tyndale.com/kids.

Visit Tracey Madder online at www.traceymadder.com.

TYNDALE is a registered trademark of Tyndale House Publishers, Inc. The Tyndale Kids logo is a trademark of Tyndale House Publishers, Inc.

The Prayer Monsters logo is a trademark of Super Faith, LLC.

Tora Fright Patches Things Up: A Story about Forgiveness

Designed by Jacqueline L. Nuñez

Edited by Sarah Rubio

Scripture quotations are taken from the *Holy Bible*, New Living Translation, copyright © 1996, 2004, 2015 by Tyndale House Foundation. Used by permission of Tyndale House Publishers, Inc., Carol Stream, Illinois 60188. All rights reserved.

Tora Fright Patches Things Up is a work of fiction. Where real people, events, establishments, organizations, or locales appear, they are used fictitiously. All other elements of the story are drawn from the author's imagination.

For manufacturing information regarding this product, please call 1-800-323-9400.

For information about special discounts for bulk purchases, please contact Tyndale House Publishers at csresponse@tyndale.com, or call 1-800-323-9400.

ISBN 978-1-4964-0872-3

Printed in China

23	22	21	20	19	18	17
7	6	5	4	3	2	1

To John, thanks for your guidance.
T. M.

ACKNOWLEDGMENTS
A special thank you to Tyndale House Publishers.
I am blessed to be part of an extraordinary team.

Tora Fright is no ordinary monster.

She lives in a tiny house at the end of Quiet Street.

But her family is not very quiet! Tora has three brothers and one sister.

Pi is the oldest, then Zeppi, then Tora's sister, R. J. Tora was the youngest for a long time, until baby Booyah was born.

Their house is often loud and messy, but Mom and Dad handle things with style.

4

6

Tora has style too. Lots of it. And today someone else has finally noticed.

"First prize!" shouts Tora, bursting through the front door. "My armadillo won first prize at the art festival!"

Tora holds up the ceramic armadillo for everyone to see. She beams with pride at the blue ribbon.

Pi helped Tora design the armadillo. He showed her how to shape it out of clay and suggested which colors to paint it. Tora added a fancy gold necklace around the armadillo's neck.

Tora brings the armadillo over to where Pi is painting. "I wouldn't have won without your help," she says, hugging him.

"No problem." Pi smiles.

9

"Congratulations, Tora!" Mom kisses Tora on the top of her head. "We are so proud of you! Let's find a special place to display your masterpiece."

Tora hands the armadillo to Mom. "Be careful with it," Tora warns.

Mom places the armadillo on the top shelf of a bookcase.

"No, not there," Tora says. "It needs to be where EVERYONE can see it!"

"How about the kitchen counter?" Mom suggests. Tora nods.

11

Tora stares at the armadillo. She readjusts it several times to make sure it looks just right. Finally satisfied, Tora heads to the living room to play a board game with Zeppi and R. J.

"Pi, do you want to play?" R. J. asks.

"No thanks," Pi replies without looking up from his painting.

But Booyah does want to play. He grabs the colorful pieces in the center of the board and shoves them into his mouth.

13

"Booyah! Stop it!" Tora hollers.

"You're messing up our game," R. J. says.

"Eww! Disgusting," Zeppi adds. He fishes the game pieces out of Booyah's slobbery mouth.

14

Booyah's lip trembles as he crawls away. He goes over to Pi's easel.

After watching Pi for a few seconds, Booyah picks up a paintbrush of his own. Tora spots him just in time.

"No, Booyah! Not on the wall!" she shouts.

Mom comes running, and Booyah drops the paintbrush. "Play with something else, Booyah," Mom says. She picks him up and sets him next to a stack of blocks in the kitchen.

16

Tora, R. J., and Zeppi continue playing their game. Tora is just about to win when she hears a huge crash. She runs to the kitchen. "My armadillo!" she cries.

17

Booyah is climbing down from the stool next to the counter. The armadillo is in pieces on the kitchen floor. "Uh-oh," Booyah says in a tiny voice.

18

"Booyah! How could you? You broke it!" Tora cries. "You always ruin everything!" She runs out of the room.

Tora hears Booyah start to cry. But she doesn't stop. She runs to her bedroom and slams the door.

Tora throws herself onto her bed and sobs into her pillow. After a moment, she hears a gentle knock on the door. Mom comes in and sits on the bed next to Tora.

20

"I'm sorry Booyah broke your armadillo," Mom says, stroking Tora's hair.
"I know how hard you worked on it."

21

Sniffling, Tora climbs onto Mom's lap. Mom holds her tight for a few minutes. "I know you want to make God happy, Tora," Mom says. "God wants us to forgive those who hurt us. He wants us to be kind even when we're upset."

Tora wipes her eyes. "I'm sorry for what I said to Booyah," she says. "He's just a baby. I know he didn't mean to break my armadillo."

Mom smiles. "What do you always remind your sister and brothers to do when they feel bad?" she asks.

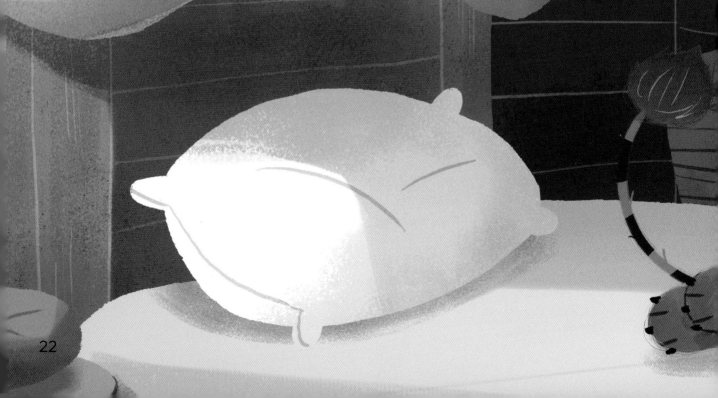

23

Tora sniffs one last big sniff. "I remind them to talk to God," she says. "I'm going to say a Prayer for Forgiveness."

Tora and Mom close their eyes and bow their heads. Tora prays,

Lord, you know that I am sad.
My little brother made me mad.
God, please help me to forgive
And in your love and kindness live.
Amen.

Mom straightens Tora's tiara. "Feeling better?" she asks.

"Almost," says Tora. "There's just one more thing I need to do." Tora grabs her big bottle of glue and runs out of her room.

Tora gives Booyah a big hug. "I'm sorry I yelled at you," she says. Booyah forgives her with a big, wet, slobbery kiss.

"Eww! Disgusting," Zeppi says. But Tora doesn't mind.

"Do you want to help me fix the armadillo?" she asks her baby brother. He nods.

Tora and Booyah sit down and glue all of the pieces of the armadillo back together. When they are finished, the armadillo does NOT look as good as new.

It looks even better!

Be kind to each other, tenderhearted,
forgiving one another, just as God
through Christ has forgiven you.

Ephesians 4:32

R. J.

R. J. loves playing sports with her brothers. Her favorite sport is soccer, and she is one of the best players in the neighborhood. R. J. never plays with dolls or wears dresses. R. J. likes to act tough, but deep inside, she has a lot of fears—until she learns to pray about them!